SUPERNATURAL RUBBER CHICKEN™

Fine Feathered Four Eyes

By
D.L. Garfinkle

Illustrated by
Ethan Long

MIRRORSTONE™

Fine Feathered Four Eyes
Supernatural Rubber Chicken™
Text ©2008 by D.L. Garfinkle
Illustrations ©2008 by Wizards of the Coast, Inc.

Published by Wizards of the Coast, Inc.

Mirrorstone, Supernatural Rubber Chicken, and their logos are trademarks of Wizards of the Coast, Inc., in the U.S.A. and other countries.

Printed in the U.S.A.

Art by Ethan Long
Book designed by Yasuyo Dunnett and Kate Irwin

First Printing

9 8 7 6 5 4 3 2 1

ISBN: 978-0-7869-5012-6
620-21861740-001-EN

Library of Congress Cataloging-in-Publication Data

Garfinkle, D. L. (Debra L.)
  Fine feathered four eyes / D.L. Garfinkle ; illustrated by Ethan Long.
    p. cm. -- (Supernatural rubber chicken)
  "Mirrorstone."
  Summary: Ed, the magical rubber chicken that lives with fourth-grade twins Lisa and Nate, continues his unique way of granting wishes for supernatural powers.
  ISBN 978-0-7869-5012-6
  (1. Magic--Fiction. 2. Wishes--Fiction. 3. Humorous stories.) I. Long, Ethan, ill. II. Title.
  PZ7.G17975Fi 2008
  (Fic)--dc22

                                                    2007045813

U.S., CANADA,
ASIA, PACIFIC, & LATIN AMERICA
Wizards of the Coast, Inc.
P.O. Box 707
Renton, WA 98057-0707
+1-800-324-6496

EUROPEAN HEADQUARTERS
Hasbro UK Ltd
Caswell Way
Newport, Gwent NP9 0YH
GREAT BRITAIN
Save this address for your records.

Visit our web site at **www.mirrorstonebooks.com**